What's Black and White and Came to Visit?

story by Evan Levine • *pictures by* Betsy Lewin

Orchard Books • New York

For Toby, who would especially like Miss Duffin — E. L.
To the 119 Tower and Ladder Company and Hooper —B.L.

Orchard Books, 95 Madison Avenue, New York, NY 10016

Manufactured in the United States of America. Printed by Barton Press, Inc.
Bound by Horowitz/Rae. Book design by Mina Greenstein.
The text of this book is set in 16 point Meridien. The illustrations are ink line and watercolor
reproduced in full color.   10 9 8 7 6 5 4 3 2 1

Library of Congress Cataloging-in-Publication Data
Levine, Evan. What's black and white and came to visit? / story by Evan Levine ; pictures by
Betsy Lewin.   p.   cm. Summary: When Lily finds a skunk in her rain gutter, the whole
town gathers round to help.
ISBN 0-531-06852-8.   ISBN 0-531-08702-6 (lib. bdg.)
[1. Skunks—Fiction.]   I. Lewin, Betsy, ill.   II. Title. PZ7.L57834Wh   1994
[E]—dc20   93-46418

One morning Lily heard a small noise under her window. It was a brushing, snuffling sort of noise, like someone sweeping with a tiny broom.

Lily went outside to the rain gutter and looked down. It was not someone sweeping with a tiny broom. It was something small and pointed and black and white, with two dark eyes.

Lily ran inside.

"Guess what's in the rain gutter?" she said to her parents.

"Rain," said her mother, who was frying bacon.

"High taxes," said her father, who was reading the paper.

"No," said Lily. "It's . . . a skunk."

Her mother stopped frying bacon. Her father stopped reading the paper.

"What's it doing?" asked her mother.

"Sitting there," said Lily.

The three of them went to peek in the rain gutter.

"What should we do with it?" asked Lily's mother.

"Why don't we call the fire department?" suggested Lily. "If they can get cats out of trees, maybe they can get skunks out of rain gutters."

"Good idea," said her mother. "I'll call."

"Did you know that skunks rarely spray their scent unless they've been threatened?" asked Lily's father, who had brought the encyclopedia.

"Hmmm," said Lily.

Lily's mother came out.

"I called the fire department," she said. "They asked if the skunk had started a fire. I said no, but they said they would come anyway."

Soon the fire engine came clanging down the block. It pulled up behind Lily's family's car in the driveway. The fire men and women spilled out. They had ladders and nets and hoses and fire extinguishers and a Dalmatian and a salami sandwich, because one of them was hungry. They were wearing noseclips, just in case.

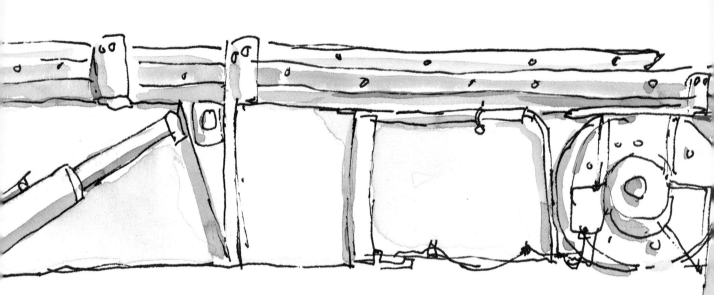

They looked in the rain gutter.

"Whoa! A skunk!" the fire chief exclaimed. Everybody moved back when Lily's father told them what the encyclopedia said.

The fire chief looked through his manual. "There's nothing about getting skunks out of rain gutters," he said. "But I have an idea. Let's make skunk noises. Maybe it'll come out."

"What kind of noises *do* skunks make?" asked Lily.

"Hmmm . . . ," said the fire chief.

The firepeople looked at one another.

"Well, maybe we should stick around, in case it starts to play with matches," the chief said.

"What about the police department?" suggested Lily.

"Another good idea," said Lily's father. "I'll call."

In a few minutes, Lily's father came out with more salami sandwiches for the firepeople.

"I called the police department," he said, over the munching. "They were disappointed when I said the skunk hadn't committed a crime, but they said they would come anyway."

Lily sat down on the grass.

"Funny thing about skunks," said her father, still reading the encyclopedia. "There are three kinds: hooded, striped, and hog-nosed. I think ours is hog-nosed."

When the police car came roaring down the street, Lily's father was talking about how a skunk's smell is really for protection. But Lily was thinking how much fun it was to sit on the grass on a cool spring morning with a skunk in the rain gutter and fire men and women on the lawn eating salami sandwiches.

The police car parked behind the fire engine, behind Lily's family's car.

The police men and women tumbled out of the police car. They had megaphones and handcuffs and whistles and walkie-talkies and a German shepherd and lemonade, because one of them was thirsty. They were holding their noses, just in case.

"My! A skunk!" the police chief said.

The police chief called the station on his walkie-talkie. "We have a 911PU—'smelly intruder on premises.'" There was static, then silence.

"They don't know what to do. We've never *had* a 911PU before," he said. "But I have an idea."

The chief pulled out his megaphone. "Okay, skunk," he boomed.

"Hog-nosed skunk," Lily's father corrected.

There was no sound from the rain gutter.

"I don't think it's going to work," said Lily.

The chief sighed. "Gee," he said. "Do you think it might like a shiny badge? Or some lemonade?"

"I think," said Lily, "that it would like to get out of the rain gutter."

"Well," said the chief, "maybe we should stick around, in case it breaks a traffic law."

Meanwhile, the policepeople and the firepeople began exchanging tips for getting salami and lemonade stains out of uniforms. Lily's father was reading about "Skydiving" because it came after "Skunk" in the encyclopedia.

"What about the mayor's office?" asked Lily.

"I don't know what the encyclopedia says about the mayor's office," said Lily's father thoughtfully. "Probably that it's an important part of town life."

"I mean," said Lily, "why don't we call the mayor's office about the skunk?"

"Yet another good idea," said her mother. "I'll call."

While she was inside, their neighbor, Miss Duffin, the Town Yodeling Expert, came over to ask what the hubbub was about.

"It's a skunk," shouted Lily.

"Hog-nosed," called her father.

"No one knows how to get it out of the rain gutter," Lily added.

"I'm sure it would come out to hear me yodel," said Miss Duffin eagerly. "People come from all over to hear me yodel."

"I don't think . . . ," Lily began. But it didn't matter what she didn't think. Miss Duffin was already yodeling loudly.

Everybody covered their ears.

Lily's mother came out of the house.

"I called the mayor's office," she shouted. "They were disappointed when I didn't know if the rain gutter was zoned for skunks, but they said the mayor would come anyway."

Lily looked around.

The police chief and the fire chief were trading sandwiches and lemonade. The police chief was saying that the fire chief wasn't giving up his full share. Lily's father was up to "Tiddlywinks" in the encyclopedia.

And everybody was offering advice.

"Hose him out!" suggested the fire chief.

"Scare him out!" yelled the police chief.

"Yodel him out!" called Miss Duffin.

A minute later, the mayor drove up in a big blue car, which had to be parked behind the police car, behind the fire engine, behind Lily's family's car.

"We hear you have a trunk in your rain gutter," she called. "If you want to keep a trunk there, you must get a permit."

"Not a trunk, a skunk," yelled Lily. "We want to know how to get it out."

The mayor looked surprised. "I need to check my rule book," she said, stepping over a fireperson snoring peacefully. "Here it is. We must have a town meeting. We will need a refreshment committee. Doughnuts are good, but some people like crullers. . . ."

"What about the skunk?" asked Lily.

"I don't know if skunks prefer doughnuts or crullers," the mayor said.

The fire chief was now suggesting loudly that they call in the National Guard. The police chief was suggesting even more loudly that everyone come to the Police Ball.

"We must call a meeting and elect skunk officials," the mayor yelled.

"No one is listening to *me*!" wailed Miss Duffin. "Everyone be quiet and let me yodel 'The Skunk Waltz.'"

Everybody was talking at the same time. It was like a fair, or a big party. It seemed that everyone had forgotten why they were there.

Lily looked at the rain gutter.

And she saw an incredible sight.

A little nose followed by two paws appeared over the side.

Then,

very slowly,

holding on very tightly,

the skunk climbed out of the rain gutter.

Lily held her breath.

The skunk looked around curiously. It looked at the yelling, eating, yodeling, sandwich-exchanging crowd. It looked at Lily. And then it scampered off into the woods behind the house.

Lily waited a moment, then carefully sniffed the air. She smiled and turned to the crowd.

"Excuse me," she called.

No one appeared to be listening.

"Excuse me," she called again, louder. "But the skunk left! It just climbed right out!"

Everybody ran over.

They gathered around the rain gutter. There was no longer anything black and white and pointed with two dark eyes.

"Well . . . I guess we did it," said the police chief uncertainly.

"That's right," the fire chief shouted. "We got it out!"

Everybody began congratulating one another.

"It was the badge," said a police man.

"It was the fire ladder," corrected a fire woman.

"It was the permit," decided the mayor.

"It was my yodeling," cried Miss Duffin.

"Hog-nosed," said Lily's father sadly.

Lily looked at everybody.

"I'm sure it was all of that," she said.

"Everyone to the town hall for doughnuts!" called the mayor. "And crullers," she added quickly.

A cheer went up as the visitors rushed for their cars.

"By the way," the mayor yelled, as she drove away, "you can keep that trunk in your rain gutter if you like."

A moment later, only Lily, her mother, her father, her father's encyclopedia, and some sandwich crusts were left on the lawn.

It was suddenly very quiet.

"I think," said Lily's mother, "that we have some cookies."

"The more I think about it, the more I'm sure it was hog-nosed," said Lily's father.

Lily's mother came out with cookies and milk and a blanket. She spread the blanket on the grass, and they sat down.

"You know, maybe it was a hooded skunk, after all," said Lily's father.

Lily and her mother smiled at each other.

And Lily thought how nice it was to sit on a quiet lawn on a cool spring morning—just the three of them.